P9-DNN-875

Wombat Divine

by MEM FOX

illustrated by

KERRY ARGENT

Harcourt Brace & Company
San Diego   New York   London

For Sue and Jane, Publishers Divine
—M. F.

For Michael,
and for Patricia and Stephen,
heartfelt thanks for your support
—K. A.

Text copyright © 1995 by Mem Fox
Illustrations copyright © 1995 by Kerry Argent

First U.S. edition 1996
First published by Omnibus Books 1995

Library of Congress Cataloging-in-Publication Data
Fox, Mem.
Wombat divine/written by Mem Fox; illustrated by Kerry Argent.
p.   cm.
Summary: Wombat auditions for the Nativity play but has trouble
finding the right part.

ISBN 0-15-201416-0

[1. Christmas—Fiction. 2. Plays—Fiction. 3. Wombats—Fiction.
4. Animals—Fiction.] I. Argent, Kerry. ill. II. Title.
PZ7.F8373Wo   1996
[Fic]—dc20   96-5480

F E D C B

Printed in Singapore

It was the week before Christmas.
Wombat loved Christmas.
He loved the carols and the candles,
the presents and the pudding,
but most of all he loved the Nativity play.

For as long as he could remember,
Wombat had wanted to be in the Nativity.
Now, at last, he was old enough to take part.
So, with his heart full of hope
and his head full of dreams,
he hurried along to the auditions.

His friends were already there.
Emu was bossing and fussing as usual.
"Now, let's get started," she said.
"Who'd like to be the Archangel Gabriel?"

"I would," said Wombat.

But he was too heavy to be the Archangel Gabriel.

Bilby was chosen instead.

Bilby patted Wombat on the back.
"Never mind, Wombat! Don't lose heart.
Why not try for a different part?"

"What a good idea," said Emu. "Now, who'd like to be Mary?"

"I would," said Wombat.

But he was too big to be Mary.

Numbat was chosen instead.

Numbat stroked Wombat's nose.
"There, there, Wombat! Don't lose heart.
Why not try for a different part?"

"Right," said Emu. "Now, who'd like to be
one of the Three Kings?"

"I would," said Wombat.

But he was too short to be a king.

The Kangaroos were chosen instead.

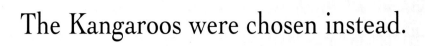

The Kangaroos put their arms around Wombat.
"Cheer up, Wombat! Don't lose heart.
Why not try for a different part?"

Wombat tried everything.

He wanted to be Joseph,

but he was too sleepy.

He wanted to be the innkeeper,
but he was too clumsy.

He wanted to be one of the shepherds,

but he was too shortsighted.

And then there were no parts left.

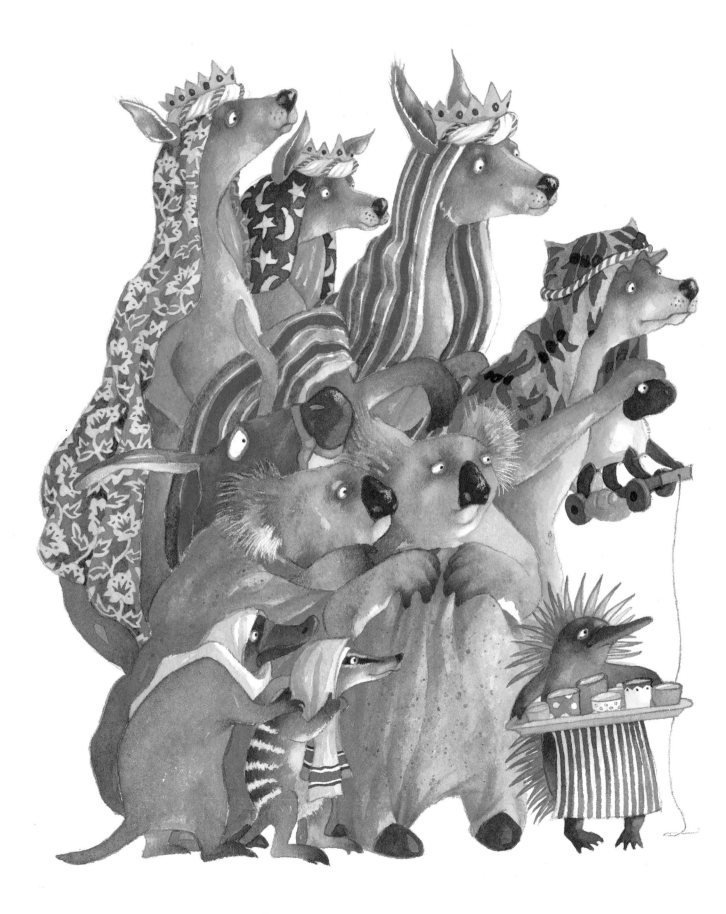

Wombat hung his head
and hoped he wouldn't cry.

Suddenly Bilby leaped into the air.
"I know!" he shouted.
"You could be the Baby Jesus!"

"Could I?" asked Wombat.
"Could I really?"

"Of course you could, Wombat," said Emu.
"Fancy my forgetting such an important part!
A Nativity without the Baby Jesus
is no Nativity at all."

Wombat was dizzy with pride.

Christmas Eve arrived at last.
Everyone was nervous except Wombat.
He lay quiet and still
throughout the whole performance.

He even fell asleep,
just as a real baby would.

On Christmas Day, when everyone was
opening presents and eating pudding,
they all agreed it had been the best Nativity ever.

"You were divine, Wombat!" said Emu.

And Wombat beamed.